OLGA

AND THE SMELLY THING FROM NOWHERE

ELISE GRAVEL is the author and illustrator of many books for children, including the Olga series, *The Mushroom Fan Club*, *The Worst Book Ever* and the Disgusting Critters series. She lives in Montreal with her husband, two daughters, and a bunch of furry monsters. www.elisegravel.com

ELISE GRAVEL

OLGA

AND THE
SMELLY THING
FROM
NOWHERE

WALKER
BOOKS

First published in Great Britain 2020 by Walker Books Ltd
87 Vauxhall Walk, London SE11 5HJ

Published by arrangement with HarperCollins Children's Books,
a division of HarperCollins, Inc.

2 4 6 8 10 9 7 5 3

This book has been typeset in Stempel Schneidler

Printed and bound by RR Donnelley Asia Printing Solutions Limited Company

British Library Cataloguing in Publication Data:
a catalogue record for this book is available from the British Library

ISBN 978-1-4063-9252-4

www.walker.co.uk

MIX
Paper from
responsible sources
FSC® C144853

HEY THERE.
I'M OLGA.

SO SMALL I CAN SEE INSIDE EVERYONE ELSE'S NOSTRILS (EWW).

SLIGHTLY GRUMPY LOOK (EVEN WHEN I'M NOT).

PERMANENT LONG-SLEEVED DRESS (I LOVE IT, OK?).

COULD EAT MAC AND CHEESE WITH PICKLES EVERY DAY.

HATE WEARING SOCKS OR SHOES!

WHAT YOU'RE ABOUT TO READ IS MY

OBSERVATION NOTEBOOK.

I like to watch stuff. All kinds of stuff. If you are weird, or a bit strange, or look like a turtle, I will watch you and write things down. I might even be watching you right now.

Just kidding. I'm not. I've got more interesting things to watch, like

Let me tell you about the cool animals I've studied.

ANIMALS ARE THE BEST.

YES WE ARE!

I LOVE ANIMALS.

All of them. I am on excellent terms with animals, except maybe mosquitoes. Animals are so much cuter than humans.

Also, animals don't pollute the planet and make wars and lie to you and steal your rubbers and call you names. They're just there, minding their own business, watching you with their big beautiful eyes, being adorable.

I LOVE ANIMALS
MY WHOLE HOUSE IS AN

MY ANIMAL
OBSERVATION LAB:

MICROSCOPE
(TO LOOK AT TINY ANIMALS)

TEST TUBES
AND FLASKS
(BECAUSE THEY
LOOK SERIOUS
AND COOL)

ANIMAL
BOOKS

TONS OF
STUFFED ANIMALS

ANIMAL
UNDERWEAR

OBSERVATION #1:

IF WE WERE TO COMPARE HUMANS AND ANIMALS IN

CUTENESS CONTESTS,

ANIMALS WOULD WIN ALL THE TIME. LET'S TAKE A LOOK AT THESE PEOPLE, FOR EXAMPLE:

THIS MAN

FIG. 1:

VS

A BUNNY

THIS WOMAN

VS

A HAMSTER

See? It's obvious. Animals are

THE CUTEST.

Even animals that people usually dislike are cuter than humans, in my humble opinion. But then some people will tell you that I have weird taste—which is perfectly fine with me, thank you very much. Nobody's forcing them to read this book.

Not too hard to pick a loser here, is it?

In case you're still not convinced that animals are cuter than humans, consider this: almost EVERYTHING ANIMALS DO IS CUTE. But if humans did the same things, it wouldn't be cute at all.

EVEN THEIR FARTS ARE CUTE.

VRUMPT

KITTY FART

PUPPY FART

FRUPP

FISH FART

P R O U T

OOPSIE!

OK, I have to admit, SOME humans are not bad. Like babies. Babies are

I would love a planet entirely populated by babies ANYTIME. Although, come to think of it, it would be a pretty weird planet.

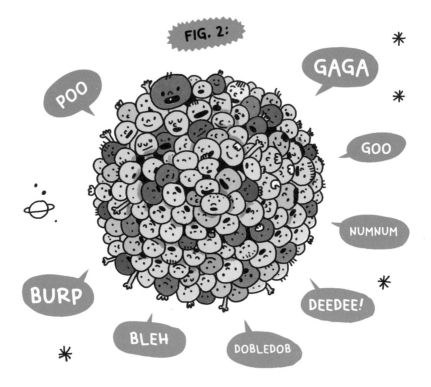

FIG. 2:

It's when they grow up that they become less cute. Look at Shalala and Farla. They're my neighbours. They think they are adorable, but they're not. All they care about is what they wear and how they do their hair, and Bip Bibop, a Korean pop star who most human girls are in love with.

But not me. I am not in love with anybody. Ew.

We've been neighbours for ever, but for as long as I can remember, they've always annoyed me.

Sometimes I wonder what it would feel like to have human friends.

Right now my closest friend is cooler than any human friend I could imagine. Her name is Rita. She's a spider who lives under the bathroom sink. She's very nice and polite, her legs are just the right length and not too hairy, and she's a very good listener.

I may not have many friends, but I am never bored. I am always very busy, and amazing things are ALWAYS happening to me. Also, I have big, big plans. I'm going to be a zoologist. A zoologist is a scientist who studies animals. I'll have a very cool lab coat, an office up a tree in the jungle, and, of course, a monkey lab assistant who I will dress up in pyjamas and name Herbert.

*TRANSLATION: GENIUS PROFESSOR OLGA, I AM SORRY TO DISRUPT YOUR VERY IMPORTANT RESEARCH, BUT YOUR MAC AND CHEESE WITH PICKLES IS READY.

I will study animals and protect them from evil humans and their pollution. Also, I will create new animals from existing species. I will probably become very famous for that. More famous than Bip Bibop, even.

FIG. 3:

KOALACTOPUS

T-CORN

SPIDHORSE

CENTICAT

HEDGEFROG

TURTLEDOG

I'll be a cool and fascinating person one day. I'll probably hang out with Jane Goodall and her chimp friends in the jungle. We'll drink tea and talk about how silly humans are.

Just wait.

2

THE

THING

Something very weird happened today while I was trying to get Rita to play Monopoly with me.

OBSERVATION #3

SPIDERS ARE VERY BAD AT BOARD GAMES. DÉSOLÉE.*

*SORRY.

I heard a noise in the rubbish bin on my back porch. I thought it might be a raccoon, and my heart leaped.

A PET RACCOON WOULD BE THE BEST!

Or maybe it was a rat! I loooooove rats. A white one with red eyes that I would name Yogurt, and I would carry her on my shoulder everywhere. The Lalas would be so jealous!

I ran to the rubbish bin but stopped myself when I had a thought: Wait a minute, maybe it was *something else*. Like maybe the rubbish bin was crawling with maggots! I've seen maggots in the rubbish bin before. Or maybe it was a dangerous burglar, hiding from the police!

OBSERVATION # 4

NEITHER OF THESE WOULD MAKE A GOOD PET.

PET BURGLAR

PET PILE OF MAGGOTS

FLB.
PLP.

What if it was MORE dangerous than a raccoon? I grabbed a broom, shielded myself with the dustpan, and gently pushed the cover of the rubbish bin aside.

SiR OLGA, KNIGHT OF NO FEAR*

BOP!

*ALMOST

Whatever it was, it was gone. The bin bags were torn up pretty badly—which was a clue indicating that this was no small animal, and certainly no maggot. Unless it was a ...

I looked around the rubbish bin and found another clue: an odd trail of poo leading towards the shed. And when I say ODD, I know what I'm talking about.

Being an observer of all things animal, I have seen many a poo in my time. On my nature expeditions, I have come across and documented:

FIG. 4:

CAT
POO

DOG
POO

BIRD
POO

FISH
POO

DEER
POO

MOUSE
POO

BUTTERFLY
POO

(YOU CAN ONLY
SEE IT WITH A
MAGNIFYING GLASS)

DR OLGA,
POO EXPERT

(OR SHOULD I SAY "POO-OLOGIST"?)

Now THIS was an entirely different kind of poo. It was the size of green peas, and shiny like marbles, but multicoloured, like Skittles.

It was the first time I'd seen:

"Well, Dr Olga," you might ask, "how can you be so sure it was poo, then?"

Well, I know, and I know with absolute certainty, because, um, it, um... smelled like poo.

OBSERVATION # 5

POO SMELLS LIKE POO.

MORE QUESTIONS?

The poo trail led right up to the shed door, which I approached on tiptoe because I'm not a fan of dark places where things might be lurking, and I didn't know what kind of thing might be in there.

That's when the mysterious poo began to glow in the dark.

Well, I don't know about you, but I declare this poo:

Maybe it was unicorn poo. What else could it be? There was only one way to know.

That was not the sound a unicorn would make, although I haven't verified that fact, so it's just a hypothesis. But in any case, I dropped my broom and ran. I love science, but I'm not ready to risk my life for it just yet. Maybe tomorrow.

The beast was right behind me, breathing down my neck. It was horrifying. I was about to be eaten alive by a creature that pooed rainbow glow-in-the-dark Skittles!

36

until I couldn't run any more because I was at the end of the alley facing a huge brick wall that I was way too small to climb.

I was trapped, and the thing was on my heels. Horrible sniffling noises were coming up right behind me. I had no choice. I had to face the beast. So I turned around and I saw...

It obviously wasn't a unicorn, nor was it a burglar or a giant mutant maggot. It looked like a cross between an inflated hamster and a potato drawn by a three-year-old.

It was looking at me with its small round eyes. It didn't look scary at all, and it didn't look scared of me. I took a few steps backwards, and it followed me.

It would be hard to look less dangerous than this thing. It even looked a bit silly, with its tongue sticking out like that. Maybe it was hungry?

I held out my hand to let it have a sniff, and it licked me!

I had never seen anything like this creature, so this was an extra-special amazing scientific encounter. Time to take out my observation notebook and note down some observations.

OBSERVATION # 6

THE THING'S BODY

It was weird looking but kind of cute. I scratched it between the ears.

Then on its back, on its chin, and on its tummy. It seemed to like it.

I picked it up and gave it a kiss on the cheek. It didn't turn into a prince or anything.

I decided that Meh was coming home with me.

3

GETTING TO KNOW MEH

Meh slept in my room all night. I tucked him into a little plastic bin next to my bed. Because I had found him in a rubbish bin, I guessed he liked it.

I used the word "slept," but it's not very accurate, because Meh:

1. **SNORES.**

RFLOOF

2. **TALKS IN HIS SLEEP.**

DOW-DOW-DOWD!

3. **SMELLS SO BAD MY WHOLE ROOM SMELLS NOW, TOO.**

So I didn't sleep much. When I "woke up" in the morning, he was standing in front of my face, showing me his behind. He seemed very proud of it.

OBSERVATION #7

MEH'S BUM LOOKS PRETTY NORMAL, LIKE A DOG'S BUM MAYBE, AND IT SMELLS JUST LIKE THE REST OF HIM.

It was Saturday, so I could spend the rest of the day studying my new companion. I followed him around with my notebook in hand. Here's a brief summary of his activities. Mostly, Meh does the following:

1 SLEEPS

RHZZZZRH.

2 RUNS AROUND LIKE A MANIAC FOR NO APPARENT REASON

DOW-DOWD.

DOW-DOWD.

3 SLEEPS AGAIN.

ZZZ.

RANDOM
OBSERVATIONS

#8 HE CROSSES HIS EYES AND LETS HIS TONGUE OUT WHEN HE'S RELAXED.

#9 HE LIKES TO BE RUBBED ON HIS TUMMY.

MEH.

#10 MY FINGERS STINK A BIT AFTER I RUB HIS TUMMY.

EWW.

MORE RANDOM OBSERVATIONS:

 #11 WHEN HE BURPS, IT SOUNDS A BIT LIKE THE WORD "RUBBER."

RUBBER.

#12 BUT HE DOESN'T SPEAK ENGLISH OR SPANISH.

WHO ARE YOU? WHERE DO YOU COME FROM? WHY DID YOU COME HERE?

DONDE ESTÁN LAS BANANAS?*

MEH?

*I DON'T REALLY SPEAK SPANISH.

#13 HE CAN GRAB STUFF WITH HIS TAIL, LIKE A MONKEY.

EWW! NOT MY TOOTHBRUSH!

MEH.

#14 HE'S NOT GOOD AT MATHS.

WHAT'S EIGHT PLUS FIVE?

RUBBER.

#15 HE'S VERY INTERESTED IN RITA, MY SPIDER FRIEND, AND I'M AFRAID HE WANTS TO EAT HER.

MEH!

BONJOUR, CHER MONSIEUR.

OMG, Meh hasn't had any food since I found him. He must be starving. But what does he EAT? Judging by the appearance of his poo, I'd have guessed Skittles, but I offered him some and he wasn't interested. I also tried:

CAT FOOD: NOPE.

MEH.

DOG FOOD: ALSO NOPE.

MEH.

FISH FOOD: NYET.

MEH-MEH.

Here's a list of the

FOODS I'VE TRIED

FOOD	VERDICT
CEREAL	NO
MILK	NO
PEANUT BUTTER	NO
CHEESE	NO
CAKE	NO
CRISPS	NO
GUM	NO
SHRIMP	NO
TOOTHPASTE	NO
SHAMPOO	NO
MAYONNAISE	NO
HOT DOGS	NO
FOOT LOTION	NO
COFFEE	NO
ICE CREAM	NO
MAC AND CHEESE WITH PICKLES	NO (I KNOW, RIGHT? INCREDIBLE!)

What did he find so appetizing in my rubbish?

Note to self: this needs to be explored further.

In the meantime, since I'm a scientist-in-training, I decided to run a series of serious science experiments, in which I found out that:

55

I ran all the experiments I could think of on Meh, and I still can't work out what species he is, or where he comes from. I looked in all my science books and I can't find anything like him.

He's not a feline or a canine, not a bunny or a pig either, although he could be a cross between the two.

He's not a reptile either, and certainly not a fish or a plant, or a mineral or a gas.

ALTHOUGH

HE SMELLS LIKE HE'S FULL OF GAS.

I'd say he's a mammal of some kind, but I can't be sure.

That's when it dawned on me.

MEH IS A NEW SPECIES!

I discovered a new species! This is most extra-ordinary. He's an unidentified mammal of the potato family. I will name the species:

OLGAMUS RIDICULUS

Why? Because I discovered it, and my name is Olga, and well, he's funny-looking. And also because it sounds like a serious scientific name for a species, and it will look better in the dictionary.

He might even come from another planet. That's highly probable, especially if we consider his glowing rainbow poo.

Maybe he was sent to Earth to collect information about us, and he communicates his findings via his tail, which looks very much like an antenna.

I'm going to write a book about him. Maybe even film a documentary. I'll probably become very famous and have my picture in newspapers and be interviewed on TV.

But observing him here at home will only get me so far. My scientific library is pretty limited.

It's time to hit the road. Meh, I'll find out who you are.

4

THE QUEST FOR TRUTH

Well, dear scientific notebook, our first expedition didn't go too well.

I took Meh for a walk and we passed Shalala and Farla on the street. Remember the Lalas? Those girls who only care about their looks?

OBSERVATION # 16

THE LALAS HAVE NO TASTE AT ALL.

They think Bip Bibop is cute. BIP BIBOP!

I can't understand that at all. Humans have such weird taste! I mean, look at him.

Those mean girls. They hurt Meh's feelings. He spent the rest of the day sleeping in the rubbish bin. Poor thing!

HE LOOKS SO

Well, Shalala and Farla are going to be sorry they made fun of Meh when they see him on TV. He's going to be more famous than Bip Bibop. Just wait and see.

People will just go crazy for him and everybody will want an Olgamus, and I'll be the only one who has one and the Lalas will be suuuuper-jealous.

I gave Meh a bath, because it's true that he is a little bit gross.

Then I made sure the Lalas were nowhere in sight, and we left for the library. I am hoping that there will be books about creatures like Meh, or clues about where he comes from.

There was, however, a little obstacle at the library door:

I noticed a sign that says that they don't allow dogs in there. Meh isn't a dog, and the sign didn't say "NO OLGAMUSES," but still, it made me nervous. And I couldn't tie Meh to a tree and leave him outside. What if he was kidnapped?

So I hid him in my backpack, and it probably looked like I was carrying a football.

He was very well behaved! He only said "Meh" every now and then, and each time I coughed to hide the sound. I hoped he wouldn't talk too much, because my throat would get sore.

First I had to sneak my way past Ms Swoop, the librarian. Ms Swoop looks a bit like a horse with her protruding front teeth. Well, a nice, punk-rock horse, with a lot of piercings and tattoos. She's always been nice to me, but I'd never done anything illegal in her library before, so I felt kind of nervous.

I passed her desk, trying to act like a perfectly normal kid who wasn't carrying a weird creature in her backpack.

Of course, that's the moment Meh chose to let out his weird panic noise.

EXCUSE ME, OLGA. ARE YOU CARRYING AN **ANIMAL** IN YOUR BAG?

UM, **NO!** I MEAN, UM...

I can't lie. I had to tell the truth.

YES, BUT I DON'T KNOW **WHAT KIND.** THAT'S WHY I'M HERE.

Ms Swoop helped me find a pile of books about weird animals and told me she'd be back in five minutes to help me during her lunch break.

I hid Meh under the table behind my huge pile and began my study.

I opened a couple of those books about weird animals, and oh wow! I have to take a break here to record this:

OBSERVATION # 17

THERE ARE SOME WEIRD GUYS ON THIS PLANET.

THE BLOBFISH

THE DUMBO OCTOPUS

DON'T DRAW ME—I'M NAKED!

THE NAKED MOLE RAT

THE YETI CRAB

75

"Any luck?" asked Ms Swoop, nearly making me jump out of my chair.

Ms Swoop's lunch break was almost over, and everybody was looking at us since Meh had screamed, so I got up and got ready to leave.

SHE THINKS MEH'S CUTE!

FINALLY

SOMEONE
WITH

TASTE!

We said goodbye to Ms Swoop and promised to come back if we found out more about Meh (and for story time on Saturdays).

For now, the library had taught us as much as it could. It was time to take Meh out into the world to see what we'd find...

5
THE DOG PARK

My next plan was to introduce Meh to other real-life animals, so I took him to the dog park. It was a nice day out, so the park was pretty full.

I love the dog park. I love to go there just to watch the dogs run around and play.

SMALL DOGS

BIG DOGS

TINY DOGS

HAIRY DOGS

LONG DOGS

FUNNY DOGS

QUIET DOGS

FANCY DOGS

UGLY DOGS

CRAZY DOGS

BARK

BARK

NOISY DOGS

DIRTY DOGS

LAZY DOGS

I took Meh out of my backpack and sat him in front of me on the ground, and immediately a couple of enormous dogs came around and began sniffing him.

(LET'S CALL THEM BRUTUS AND BADDUS.)

I was sure that these huge dogs would swallow Meh whole, and I started regretting having brought Meh to the park, when he started taking a deep breath:

He was puffing up like a giant puffer fish! He got really, really big and started emitting a screechy noise, like an inflated balloon that's leaking air.

The big dogs lowered their ears and slunk away, whimpering all the way to their owners' sides. Now all the dogs in the park were eyeing Meh with fear. All except one.

This weird tiny dog was not at all put off by Meh.

He trotted up to Meh, smelled his bum for a while, and then peed at his feet.

Then Meh and the tiny dog started chasing each other around like puppies.

Then this kid appeared by my side. "His name is Mister," he said. He had a haircut that looked like an angry kid had drawn it. The kid, not the dog.

Then Mister started to pee in circles around Meh, which didn't seem to bother Meh one bit.

"I know he's a dog," the kid said, "but I have a hard time believing he evolved from a wolf.

"I think he might also have chipmunks somewhere in his ancestry."

ANATOMY OF MISTER

FIG. 1.2.3

OH, ISN'T IT ADORABLE! A POTATO AND A RAT SITTING IN A TREE, K-I-S-S-I-N-G.

HA-HA! LOOK AT THAT GUY'S HAIRCUT!

?

Yep, it was the Lalas again, sniggering at us from the other side of the fence.

YUCK, YUCK!

IGNORE THEM, THEY'RE SO RUDE. I'M OLGA, BY THE WAY.

CHUCK. NICE TO MEET YOU.

Chuck was a nice human being. He was as nice as an animal. Like Ms Swoop. I was trying to imagine which animal Chuck would be when Meh started doing his weird noise again.

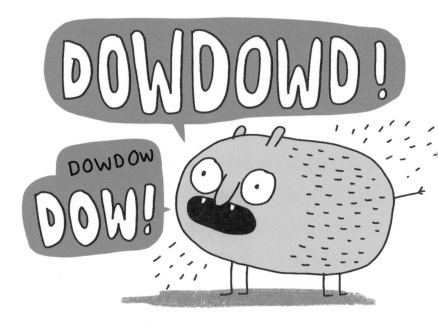

"Why is he doing that?" said Chuck. "Is he hungry?"

Uh-oh. Meh still hadn't eaten anything in two days.

I needed to get him something to eat fast.

6

STUFF 'N' THINGS 'N' MORE!

MEH IS PROBABLY DYING OF STARVATION. WHAT A HORRIBLE PET OWNER I AM!

I tried everything I could find around my house. Where could I find foods that an Olgamus would like?

I knew just the place. It was some kind of corner shop, but, in fact, it was much more than that. It was called:

Mr Hoopah, the owner of the shop, was a pretty nice man. He had the face of a turtle, with a long, skinny body, but with a very round tummy, as though he had just swallowed a basketball.

Mr Hoopah's corner shop was hard to describe. There were so many strange things in there, you could get lost, even though it was tiny.

YOU WILL FART **38** TIMES TOMORROW.

PLASTIC
FORTUNE-TELLING
BROCCOLI PLANTS

MEAT LOAF

SCRATCH-AND-SNIFF
NAIL POLISH

GLOW-IN-THE-DARK
TOILET BRUSH

BORA THE EXPLODER

BORA THE EXPLODER
FOOT MASSAGER

LIGHT-UP MUSICAL
LITTER BOX

HUMAN-SIZED
PEANUT BUTTER JAR

BIP BIBOP
PLASTERS

LIVE FLIES IN A CAN

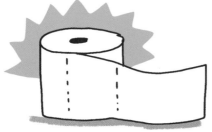

NACHO-SCENTED
TOILET PAPER

"Hello, wonderful customer!" said Mr Hoopah as I walked in. "Hey, it's my favourite one, Miss Olga! What brings you here this afternoon?"

I took Meh out of my backpack, and Mr Hoopah's jaw dropped.

"It's an *Olgamus Ridiculus*," I explained. "A new species that I discovered. He hasn't eaten anything in days because I can't find anything he likes. He must be famished, or worse: DYING! Can you help me find out what he eats?"

"Well, adorable customer, you haven't tried every-thing then. Wait a minute—I'll be right back."

He disappeared behind a back-of-the-shop door that no customer in history has ever been allowed to enter.

Finally, Mr Hoopah stepped through the doors looking hot and tired and carrying an armful of foods I
had never seen on the shelves.

One by one, he opened a package or jar and placed it in front of Meh.

"This animal is extremely odd indeed," said Mr Hoopah. "How can anyone not like dried pimple mushrooms? Mmm! They are my favourite!"

Mr Hoopah looked discouraged, so I picked Meh up and was about to leave when Meh started freaking out in my arms.

He jumped out of my arms, ran like I'd never seen him run, and then jumped on the counter, ending up face-first in a bowl of olives that Mr Hoopah always offers his customers.

"I think we have a winner!" exclaimed Mr Hoopah, watching the Olgamus stuff his face with olives. "Nobody ever wants my olives. I'm glad someone does!"

And did he ever enjoy them!

Meh was still tearing through the olive bowl when Mr Hoopah's door chime rang. In walked the Lalas.

"Fart balloon?" Oh, how the Lalas get on my nerves!!!

OBSERVATION # 19

THE LALAS ARE BAD FOR MY FINGERNAILS.

The Lalas went to the magazine rack and started leafing through the latest copy of *Twerp Girl* magazine, which is the only thing they read.

I'LL HAVE TO READ ONE OF THOSE SOMEDAY. TO STUDY THEM, I MEAN. AS A SCIENTIST.

Meh had finished the bowl of olives and was off somewhere.

I found him napping on a pile of boxes of sauerkraut-flavoured corn flakes.

I bought five jumbo jars of olives from Mr Hoopah, picked up Meh, and left. Meh went all limp and soft in my arms.

I'm in love. Isn't he absolutely adorable?

7

"OLGA THE chef"

The weather was nice, so I plopped Meh in his little rubbish bin on the front porch and left him there to nap.

HE'S **SO** CUTE!

Then I came inside to write everything I've been learning about Meh. I haven't written any new observations in a while and there's a lot of catching up to do, so here goes:

SCIENCE UPDATE

#21 THE OLGAMUS'S DIET CONSISTS OF **OLiVES.**

#22 THE OLIVE STONES MIGHT EXPLAIN THE SHAPE OF HIS POO, BUT THEY DO NOT EXPLAIN THE RAINBOW COLOUR.

#23 HE'S ABSOLUTELY ADORABLE AND I LOVE HIM AND HE'S **NOT A FART BALLOON!**

#24 THE LALAS ARE THE MOST ANNOYING CREATURES ON EARTH.

Now that I know what Meh likes to eat, I want to demonstrate my love for him by preparing a delicious recipe. Delicious for olgamuses, I imagine. My culinary creation is called

OLIVE potage

"AUX QUATRE OLIVES" *

INGREDIENTS:

OLIVES
OLIVE JUICE
OLIVE OIL
OLIVE PASTE
CHOCOLATE (FOR TASTE)

*NOTE: RECIPES, LIKE SPIDERS, SOUND MORE SOPHISTICATED IN FRENCH.

It's gross and it smells horrible, but you should probably write it down in case you find an Olgamus yourself one day.

I'm pretty proud of my recipe, and I think that on top of becoming a famous zoologist, I'd like to become an animal chef as well. I'll probably even have my own TV show.

It took me about an hour to clean up all the olive mush and olive stones on the kitchen floor, and I just have to say:

OBSERVATION # 25

COOKING IS FUN, **BUT** I **HATE** CLEANING UP AFTER MYSELF.

But the soup was ready. I poured it into my favourite porcelain bowl, and I was taking it to Meh outside on the porch so he could have a little picnic.

Oh no!!!

EMERGENCY BROADCAST:

I JUST WENT OUTSIDE
AND MEH IS **NOT**
IN HIS RUBBISH BIN
ANY MORE!

I looked in my back porch rubbish bin, under the porch, on the pavement, in the bushes around the porch, and up the nearest tree: Meh was nowhere to be seen.

OBSERVATION # 26

PEOPLE TEND TO ACT SURPRISED WHEN YOU YELL "MEEH" AT THE TOP OF YOUR LUNGS FOR FIFTEEN MINUTES.

WHERE IS MY OLGAMUS ???

I spent the whole night imagining horrible things happening to my poor, sweet Meh.

WHAT IF HE'S BEEN ABDUCTED BY **ALIENS?**

WHAT IF HE'S BEEN KIDNAPPED BY AN EVIL WITCH WHO WANTS TO COOK HIM FOR DINNER?

WHAT IF HE'S **LOST?**

WHAT IF SOMEONE MISTOOK HIM FOR A **POTATO** AND ATE HIM?

WHAT IF HE GOT TOO FULL OF **GAS** AND FLOATED AWAY?

WHAT IF SOME KIDS ARE PLAYING WITH HIM LIKE HE'S A **FOOTBALL?**

Or worse: What if he's been unhappy with me? What if he's left because he's found more interesting friends? What if he's angry at me for performing all those science experiments on him, like the baby pyjamas and everything? I remember now that he was not exactly pleased with that one.

I didn't sleep at all. I got up at five in the morning. The olive soup bowl sat on the porch, untouched.

THE SADDEST
BOWL OF
OLIVE SOUP

EVER.

8

THE

QUEST

This morning, I walked some more around the block, but there was still no sign of Meh. I looked everywhere. In the bushes, under cars, behind people's sheds, under porches.

He couldn't have walked that far. With his tiny stick legs, he only walked about a mile a day. There was no way he could have taken a bus, or a plane. I didn't think they'd let him on a plane anyway since he had no passport (that I knew of). I hear that the airport police are pretty

SUSPiCiOUS

OF ANYTHING STRANGE.

(THIS *WOULD* APPEAR STRANGE TO A NORMAL PERSON.)

AIRPORT POLICE

RUBBER.

I thought that maybe he went back to one of the places we visited together. Like the library. So I went and saw Ms Swoop at her desk.

LET'S MAKE A
LOST PET SIGN!

She gave me a marker and some paper and I got to work. "We can use the library's photocopier when you're done."

Here's what I came up with. Not bad for someone drawing from memory, huh? Maybe I'll be a zoologist--chef-artist when I'm older.

LOST
OLGAMUS

- LOOKS LIKE A FURRY FOOTBALL
- SMELLS BAD (BUT THAT'S NO REASON TO MAKE FUN OF HIM)
- SAYS "MEH" ALL THE TIME
- LOVES OLIVES
- IS UNBEARABLY CUTE

IF FOUND
CALL OLGA 555-5555

Ms Swoop took my poster, went off to the library office, and came back with fifty copies and a stapler.

We went off through the neighbourhood putting up our signs as we went. I had a few copies left when we showed up in front of Mr Hoopah's shop.

"Mr Hoopah has a notice board next to the front door," I said. "Let's ask him if we can put up a sign there."

"Good idea," said Ms Swoop. "Maybe I'll get something to eat as well."

Mr Hoopah was happy to see me, and he let me put up my sign on his board.

Mr Hoopah read my sign and looked sad to learn that I had lost Meh.

TAKE THESE, PERFECT CUSTOMER! THEY'RE **THE BEST OLIVES IN THE WORLD**, SPECIAL IMPORTATION. THEY ARE MARINATED IN **HERRING OIL**. HOPEFULLY THEY'LL HELP YOU FIND YOUR **OLGAMUS**.

THANK YOU, MR HOOPAH!

OLIVES

Mr Hoopah's present made me want to cry a little. And then Ms Swoop shrieked.

"Mr Hoopah! You've got dried pimple mushrooms! I can't find those anywhere. They're my favourite!"

Mr Hoopah beamed. "Aren't they absolutely exquisite? I'm happy to finally meet a customer who can appreciate true delicacies."

Mr Hoopah and Ms Swoop smiled at each other for a long awkward moment.

OBSERVATION # 27

EWWW.

ADULTS ARE WEIRD.

We left Mr Hoopah's shop with my jar of olives, and Ms Swoop had to go back to work, so we said good-bye. Then I thought it would be a good idea to lay out an olive trail in the nearby alleys leading back to my house. Then I ran into Chuck and his "dog," Mister.

We laid olive trails everywhere, and then we sat on my porch to think. Where could Meh possibly be?

We racked our brains but we still had no idea, so I went inside to get us some ice cream cones, because I'm pretty sure that...

OBSERVATION # 28

ICE CREAM MAKES YOUR BRAIN SHARPER.

It worked, because Chuck had an idea.

MAYBE HE JUST WENT BACK TO WHERE HE CAME FROM?

I used my very best *Star Battle* stationery and wrote:

STAR BATTLE

DEAR MEH,

I HOPE YOU DIDN'T LEAVE EARTH BECAUSE OF THE SCIENCE EXPERIMENTS I DID ON YOU. I AM SO SORRY.

PLEASE COME BACK. I LOVE YOU. I PROMISE I WILL TAKE GOOD CARE OF YOU AND FEED YOU TONS OF OLIVES.

WE COULD EVEN GO ON A TRIP TO GREECE. THEY HAVE DELICIOUS OLIVES THERE.

PLEASE COME HOME SOON. I MISS YOU SO MUCH.

OLGA

I added a few glittery butterfly stickers, put the letter in an envelope, and thought about how to send it to outer space. That was the tricky part.

Chuck and I came up with a couple of ideas:

WE COULD SHOOT THE LETTER USING A **HUGE SLINGSHOT.**

OR PUT IT IN THE **MAIL** WITH "OUTER SPACE" AS THE ADDRESS.

OUTER SPACE

OR SEND IT TO ASTRONAUT **CHRIS HADFIELD** AND ASK HIM TO BRING IT ON HIS NEXT TRIP, BUT THAT WOULD TAKE A WHILE.

CHRIS HADFIELD

OR ATTACH IT TO A **SMALL ROCKET.** MAYBE MR HOOPAH SELLS SOME. HE SELLS **EVERYTHING.**

We went to Mr Hoopah's shop and explained our plan, but, unbelievably, he didn't have mini-rockets in his shop.

He went to his storeroom and came out with this pretty huge pig-shaped one. Mr Hoopah inflated it to the max and sold it to us for a pound, which is a very good price for a Giant Super-Huge Biggo-Jumbo Megaballoon.

We went to the park, attached the letter to the Giant Super-Huge Biggo-Jumbo Megaballoon, and let it go.

"Maybe Mister can help," Chuck said. "He may not be much to look at, but he has a very good sense of smell. Maybe HE can find Meh."

THE LEAST CREDIBLE DETECTIVE DOG EVER.

"Good idea!" I said. "Does he need something from Meh to pick up his scent? I have just the thing. Give me a minute."

I returned with Meh's "bed," or rubbish bin, which I hoped was still holding his scent. I gave it to Chuck.

HERE, BOY! SMELL THIS!

Mister ran up to the bin, peed, sniffed it, peed again as if to say "Got it," and started running.

He seemed to have picked up a scent and was trotting down the road. Chuck and I followed him, me holding the rubbish bin, Chuck holding the jar of olives.

Mister took us around the neighbourhood, stopping to sniff posts and trees and peeing on each and every one of them.

OBSERVATION # 29

MISTER CHASING A REAL BANDIT WOULD BE FUN TO WATCH.

PLEASE, WAIT A SEC, SIR, THERE'S SOMETHING I **NEED** TO DO.

We passed the library and the dog park, and stopped exactly (I counted) sixty-four times for Mister to pee.

MISTER'S CHASING TECHNIQUE:

1 RUN
2 PEE
3 RUN
4 PEE

Then I got very excited when Mister stopped next to a public waste bin, but it was only because Mister had found half a rotten tuna sandwich.

EWWWWW!
HE'S PEEING AND EATING
AT THE SAME TIME!

BLARF BLORG.

We ran and ran through the whole neighbourhood. I'm drawing a map here just because I like to draw maps.

And then Mister stopped running, almost in front of my house. In fact, he was in front of my neighbours' house.

The Lalas, remember the Lalas?

The überannoying Lalas?

We climbed the steps after Mister and rang.

SHE?

The Lalas ran inside the house and I heard them giggling (their speciality) and then opening and closing doors. It felt like hours, but finally they came back, holding a giant basket.

And inside the basket, there was...

THAT **CAN'T** BE MEH!

YES IT IS! SHE WAS SO UGLY, POOR THING. WE GAVE HER A **BEAUTY MAKEOVER.** NOW SHE COULD BE ON THE COVER OF *TWERP GIRL* MAGAZINE!

I carefully removed the sunglasses.

MEH.

IT WAS MEH
ALL RIGHT!

He looked totally ridiculous, dressed up like that and smelling like the perfume section of a department store, but it was him, alive and healthy!

I must admit I was ashamed of having missed such crucial information. That's not very professional. So I'm noting it down right away:

OBSERVATION # 30

MY OLGAMUS IS A FEMALE.

Phew, this has been a very emotional day. I need to spend some quiet time alone with Meh. So I said goodbye to the Lalas, Mister, and Chuck, came back home, and fed Meh a big bowl of olive soup (which he loved).

Then I lined his little rubbish bin with fresh, clean tissue paper.

MEH'S LITTLE
PARADISE.

I have to admit that he doesn't look too unhappy after his trip to the Lalas'. I mean SHE. SHE doesn't look too unhappy. Woah! That will take me a while to get used to.

9

SOME HUMANS

We spent a quiet night resting from our trauma, and this morning I took my time performing a "reverse makeover" to undo the damage the Lalas had done. I can't see why suddenly being female is a reason to look like a pink prize poodle.

HOW TO DO A
REVERSE
MAKEOVER:

(I SHOULD SUBMIT THIS ARTICLE TO *TWERP GIRL* MAGAZINE)

1. REMOVE
SILLY BOW

2. TAKE BATH
TO REMOVE PINK DYE
AND PERFUME

3. COMB OUT
UGLY PERM

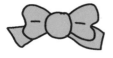

4. LEAVE NAIL POLISH
BECAUSE IT'S
KIND OF COOL

I dried him off, I mean her, and gave her a big hug.
I LOVE HER SO MUCH SO MUCH SO MUCH! I'm so
happy he's back. I mean she.

I'm so happy I'm thinking of throwing a big party.

Well, this didn't take too long as I had a pretty small guest list. There was Ms Swoop the librarian, Chuck and Mister (note to self: don't forget to "pee-proof" the floor with newspapers), and Mr Hoopah from the corner shop.

But what should I do about the Lalas? I don't feel like inviting them, but they seem to have been extra nice to Meh.

INVITING THE LALAS?

PROS	CONS
• THEY'RE FRIENDS WITH MEH.	• THEY'RE ANNOYING
• THEY REVEALED IMPORTANT INFOR-MATION.	• THEY'RE ANNOYING
• THEY'RE MY NEIGHBOURS.	• THEY'RE ANNOYING
• I'M A NICE PERSON.	• THEY'RE . . .

All right, all right, I'm inviting them.

I've got things to do now; be back tomorrow for an update. This is my first party. I am very stressed.

As promised, here's a brief summary of the party:

OBSERVATION # 31

PARTIES ARE FUN.

Mr Hoopah brought some zit mushrooms, cauliflower chips, and onion-flavoured pop. Luckily, I had prepared some mac and cheese with pickles beforehand.

Ms Swoop danced with Mr Hoopah, and Chuck gave us an air-guitar performance.

I introduced everybody to Rita, my spider, and Chuck
fed her some fish flakes, which she seemed to like.

Oh, and then the Lalas did something that took me by
surprise! They had brought a few sheets of paper with
writing and diagrams on them, which they handed
to me.

It was a compilation of their own observations of Meh, and there was lots of stuff I didn't know. They had done a good job!

Of course it wasn't exactly zoologist quality, but not bad for kids who only read *Twerp Girl* magazine.

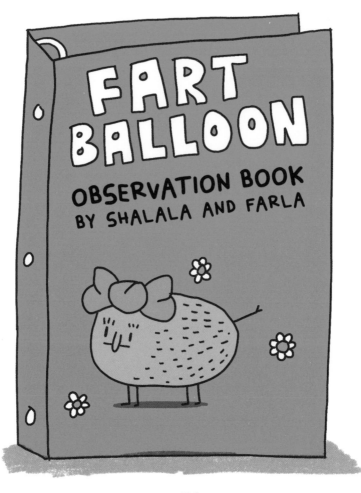

SHE'LL FALL ASLEEP IF YOU **READ HER A BOOK.**

Z.

ZZZ.

SHE ONLY SLEEPS FACING **THE NORTH POLE.**

SHE LIKES TO LICK PEBBLES.

SLURP SLURP

MEH? MEH? MEH?

SHE TRIES TO COMMUNICATE WITH **FLIES.**

OH BABY, LET'S PLAY MONOPOLY!

SHE **DANCES** WHEN WE PLAY BIP BIBOP.

MEEH! MEH!

The rest of the guests helped me clean up, except maybe Mister, who, instead of helping, decided to pee a couple of times on the kitchen floor before leaving.

When everybody was gone, I couldn't find Meh. I panicked for a few moments until I found her stuffed in her rubbish bin, her belly full of olives.

BLORF ROFL FRLZ RZLP PRLPT RUBBER

A STUFFED OLGAMUS IS A HAPPY OLGAMUS

Before going to sleep, I thought about the party and my new friends. I decided that even though animals are still the coolest creatures ever...

OBSERVATION # 32

SOME HUMANS ARE OK AFTER ALL.

MEH & OLGA: THE SCRAPBOOK!

(BECAUSE I DON'T LIKE TO WASTE PAPER)

MEH
+
OLGA
4
EVER

STORY TIME!

AT THE SCIENCE MUSEUM

OLGA'S *famous* OLIVE MUFFINS *recipe!*

- 85g SLICED PITTED OLIVES
- 60g CHOPPED FETA CHEESE
- 75g FINELY SLICED SPRING ONION
- 60ml EXTRA VIRGIN OLIVE OIL
- 225ml MILK
- 1 EGG
- 210g SELF-RAISING FLOUR (SIEVED)

1. PREHEAT THE OVEN TO 200 DEGREES C / GAS MARK 6.
2. PUT ALL THE INGREDIENTS IN A BIG BOWL. STIR BRIEFLY (BUT NOT TOO MUCH).
3. USE A SPOON TO PLACE MIXTURE INTO MINI MUFFIN TINS. BAKE FOR ABOUT 10 MINUTES OR UNTIL COOKED.

THE SCIENTIFIC METHOD

OR WHAT TO DO IF YOU THINK YOU'VE DISCOVERED A NEW SPECIES.

1 OBSERVATION

HMM, INTERESTING.

2 QUESTION

WHAT IS IT?

3 RESEARCH

IT'S NOT A POTATO, IT'S NOT A BEAVER . . .

DATA: NO ANSWER FROM OUTER SPACE